For Toby, Isla and Jesse — A.D.

For my father — V.S.

First published 2013 by Walker Books Ltd, 87 Vauxhall Walk, London SE11 5HJ • This edition published 2014 • 10 9 8 7 6 5 4 3 2 1 • Text © 2013 Alexis Deacon • Illustrations © 2013 Viviane Schwarz • The right of Alexis Deacon and Viviane Schwarz to be identified as author and illustrator respectively of this work has been asserted by them in accordance with the Copyright, Designs and Patents Act 1988 • This book has been typeset in Franklin Gothic Extra Condensed • Printed in China • All rights reserved. No part of this book may be reproduced, transmitted or stored in an information retrieval system in any form or by any means, graphic, electronic or mechanical, including photocopying, taping and recording, without prior written permission from the publisher. • British Library Cataloguing in Publication Data: a catalogue record for this book is available from the British Library • ISBN 978-1-4063-5266-5 • www.walker.co.uk

WALKER BOOKS
AND SUBSIDIARIES
LONDON • BOSTON • SYDNEY • AUCKLAND

CHEESE BELONGS TO YOU!

Alexis Deacon illustrated by **Viviane Schwarz**

THIS IS RAT LAW:

cheese belongs to **you.**

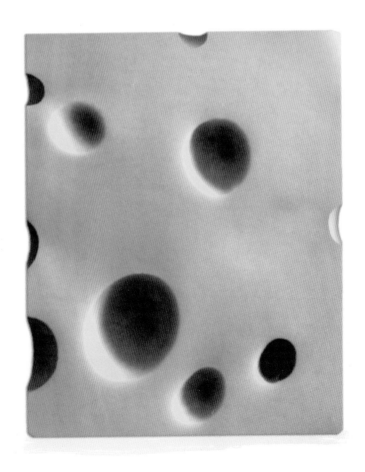

Unless a **big** rat wants it.
Then cheese belongs to them.

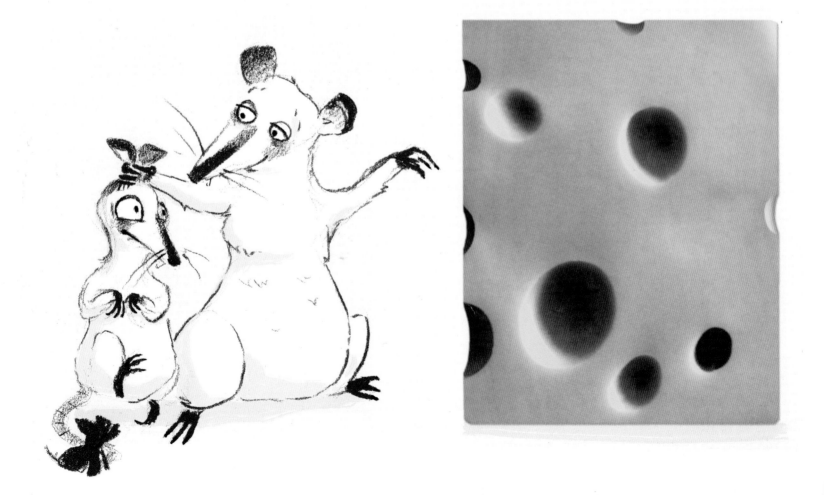

Unless a **bigger** rat wants it.
Then cheese belongs to them.

Unless a quicker rat wants it . . .

or a **stronger** rat wants it …

or a **scary** rat …

or a **hairy** rat ...

or a dirty, hairy, scary rat . . .

or a big, quick, strong, scary, hairy, dirty rat.

If a big, quick, strong, scary, hairy, dirty rat wants it, then **cheese** belongs to them.

Unless a gang of rats wants it.

Unless a gang of big, quick, strong, scary, hairy, dirty rats wants it.

Unless the biggest gang of the biggest, quickest, strongest, scariest, hairiest, dirtiest rats wants it.

Unless the boss of the biggest, quickest, strongest, scariest, hairiest, dirtiest rats wants it.

If the boss of the biggest, quickest, strongest, scariest, hairiest, dirtiest rats wants it, then cheese belongs to them.

Unless . . .

someone else **wants** to be boss.

if you still want it. **THAT IS RAT LAW.**

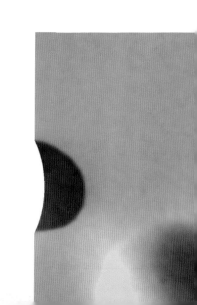

PLEASE!